This book is to be returned on or before the last date stamped below

or by phone 08458 247 200

MARWOOD
THE LION & THE
MOUSE

Libraries & Archives

W
FRANKLIN WATTS

First published in 2009 by
Franklin Watts
338 Euston Road
London
NW1 3BH

Franklin Watts Australia
Level 17/207 Kent Street
Sydney
NSW 2000

Text © Franklin Watts 2009
Illustration © Anni Axworthy 2009

A CIP catalogue record for this book is available
from the British Library.

ISBN 978 0 7496 8527 0 (hbk)
ISBN 978 0 7496 8533 1 (pbk)

Series Editor: Jackie Hamley
Series Advisor: Dr Hilary Minns
Series Designer: Peter Scoulding

Printed in China

Franklin Watts is a division of
Hachette Children's Books,
an Hachette Livre UK company.
www.hachettelivre.co.uk

This kind of story is called a fable. It was written by a Greek author called Aesop over 2,500 years ago. Fables are stories that can teach something. Can you work out what the lesson in this fable might be?

One day, a tiny
mouse woke Lion up.

Lion was cross.
He caught Mouse
and was about to
eat him when ...

Mouse squeaked, "Don't eat me. I might be able to help you one day."

7

"How can a tiny mouse help me?" laughed Lion. But he let Mouse go.

Soon after, Lion got stuck in a net.

11

Days passed and Lion got weaker. Then ...

13

Mouse squeaked,
"Can I help you, Lion?"

"I'm stuck!" cried Lion.

Mouse nibbled and
nibbled until Lion
was free.

"Thank you, Mouse!"
purred Lion.

Puzzle Time!

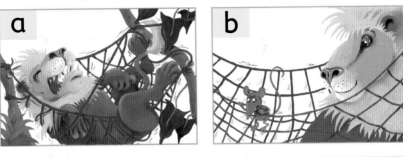

a

b

c

d

e

f

Put these pictures in the right order and tell the story!

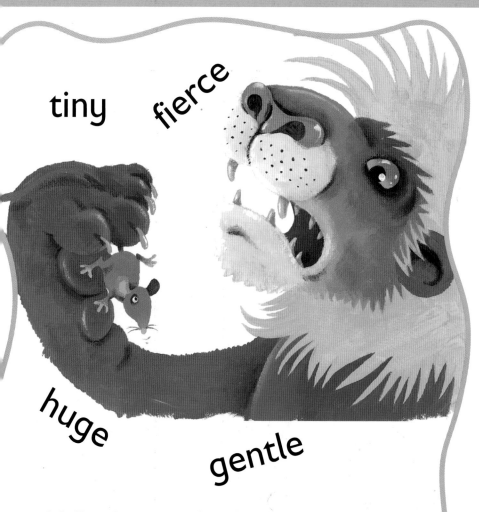

tiny　　fierce

huge

gentle

Which words describe Lion
and which describe Mouse?

Turn over for answers!

Notes for adults

TADPOLES are structured to provide support for newly independent readers. The stories may also be used by adults for sharing with young children.

Starting to read alone can be daunting. **TADPOLES** help by providing visual support and repeating words and phrases. These books will both develop confidence and encourage reading and rereading for pleasure.

If you are reading this book with a child, here are a few suggestions:

1. Make reading fun! Choose a time to read when you and the child are relaxed and have time to share the story.
2. Talk about the story before you start reading. Look at the cover and the blurb. What might the story be about? Why might the child like it?
3. Encourage the child to retell the story, using the jumbled picture puzzle as a starting point. Extend vocabulary with the matching words to characters puzzle.
4. Discuss the story and see if the child can relate it to their own experience, and perhaps think about the moral of the fable.
5. Give praise! Remember that small mistakes need not always be corrected.

Answers

Here is the correct order!
1. d 2. c 3. f 4. a 5. b 6. e

Words to describe Mouse:
gentle, tiny

Words to describe Lion:
fierce, huge